THE AULD MITHER

William Meikle

THE AULD MITHER

George Duncan was getting impatient. He'd spent three sleepless nights getting this presentation together, a last gasp attempt to keep the company afloat, and his people in work.

It's not my fault if they're too dumb to know that their own livelihoods depend on this.

"If I could have your attention please," he said, trying not to let his irritation show. "I think we're ready to begin."

They'd already been there for twenty minutes, chatting, drinking coffee, discussing the *fucking* weather -- it's Scotland, it's wet, deal with it -- anything other than focus on the task at hand. It wasn't as if they hadn't spent months talking about it - the need for modernisation and efficiency to bring prosperity to this small town on the edge of the Highlands; an attempt to stop the flow of jobs and money to the bigger cities and prevent the slow fall into shortbread-tin tourism that afflicted much of the rest of the North. He'd tried to impress on them all the importance of the meeting. But here they were, the same country hicks they'd always been, more interested in rain and wind than the future of the company.

Maybe I should just sack the lot of them, sell up and run.

It was looking more desirable with each passing day. But George Duncan was a businessman, and he had his pride. This latest idea had been run past his bankers, his silent partners, and several of the richer patrons of the local golf club. If he backed down now it would diminish him in the eyes of powerful men, and he couldn't have that.

"Please?" he said, motioning the other board members to their seats. The tone of his voice brooked no disobedience, and this time they all sat in their places.

He allowed himself a small smile.

It's showtime.

He used a remote control unit to dim the lights until only the projected screen on the wall provided any light. The other four were now little more than shadowy figures around the table.

"I've brought you here for the final decision," George began. "I'm not prepared to hang around on this any longer. I'm pushing on with the expansion plan."

As he knew she would, Sheena Davis interrupted almost immediately.

"I thought we agreed to wait?"

She was a *whiner*. George hated her with a vengeance, but when he had bought this business, it had been from her family, and one of the conditions was that she would be on the board. He didn't have to like her though.

"Wait for what?" George replied sarcastically. "Christmas?"

The woman's whine got louder. She sounded just like one of the animals out in the pen, always bleating and whining, even when they were well fed, well looked after. Like the beasts, the Davis woman didn't know how lucky she was.

And like the beasts, I'll just have to show her who's Boss.

"We decided to test the market first..." she continued.

George nipped it in the bud fast.

"No. There's no time for that. I know this business. I've been a butcher all my life. And this is my company, when push comes to shove."

"And we don't get a say?" The whine was full strength now and George was rapidly losing patience. He fought to keep his temper, and replied as evenly as he was able.

"Not on this, no."

"I'm not sure I like that," the Davis woman said. Even although it was too dark in the room to see, George could imagine the supercilious smirk on the woman's face. She had come from old money, and never let George forget his own humble beginnings in a shop in Derbyshire. His calm finally snapped and his voice rose.

"I'm not sure I give a fuck."

He had to imagine the shock on her face, but some of it was more than evident in her voice.

"I've never been so insulted."

George laughed.

"You need to get out more."

He paused and spoke softly, but the room had fallen so quiet there was no way that they couldn't hear him. "You all know where the door is. Does anybody want to leave?"

Nobody moved from the table. The Davis woman *sniffed* loudly, just to let him know she wasn't happy, but he knew he had her -- he had them all.

"Thank you," he said, and threw them a bone. "Don't worry. You'll find I've put some thought into it."

He brought up the first screen. It showed a graph with steadily increasing growth against time. George slipped into his singsong presentation voice. He was happier now. He'd practised this bit, and if there was one thing he knew well, it was how to sell an idea.

"My projected figures show that with an increased throughput of two hundred per cent, we can increase profits nearly fivefold. If you'll just..."

Something *scraped*, like fingernails on a blackboard. A shadow passed in front of the screen, a bent and mangled hand with long taloned fingers.

George was stopped in mid-flow. It didn't improve his temper any.

"Who did that? Stop playing silly buggers!"

A bulky shadow moved across in front of the projector,

something misshapen, but very fast. Somebody -- one of the women - screamed.

Blood sprayed in the air and splattered across the projected screen.

There was a shocked silence for two beats, then louder screams pierced the quiet - this time both male and female. There was a frenzy of activity in the dark room. Chairs were knocked over and there was another scream as bones *cracked* under a heavy footfall. A body was thrown against a wall, the crash shaking the whole room before falling to the floor like a puppet after its strings had been cut.

Through all this George had stood still, unable to take in what was happening around him, afraid to move unless the chaos around him swallowed him as well.

Silence fell in the boardroom - but only for a second. A moist *ripping* sound, too loud in the dark, filled the space. George tasted blood and smelled the same acrid tang of fear that he knew all too well from the beasts he'd had under his knife over his years in the trade.

Something glowed luminescent blue and shadows ran across the walls. A body passed in front of the projector and knocked it sideways to a skewed angle.

One final scream gave way to dead silence.

George sidled around, back pressed hard against a wall, left hand feeling along, hoping against hope that he'd find the door handle. Instead his hand touched something warm -- warm and wet. He smelled blood, the coppery tang almost making him gag. Before he could try to move again something hard and cold pressed against his ribcage.

"Butchery is it?" a soft voice said. "Let me show you where butchery gets you."

He had a moment when he felt something cold slice through clothes, flesh and fat. His lower torso and legs felt wet and warm, but George felt empty inside.

He was dead before he hit the floor.

The last thing he saw was blood running down the screen,

partly obscuring the slide he'd spent so long preparing - the one which read: ABATTOIR: PROPOSED ENLARGEMENT.

~-oOOOo-~

Lucy Duncan had finally decided to tell Dave how their father died.

About time too - I thought I was going to get the cold shoulder for the whole trip.

The journey had proved to be a nightmare so far. The train was full, so full that although they were travelling first class, they were sharing the compartment with a horde of others - students, squaddies and oilmen, all of them drunk, half drunk or intending to get that way. The buffet car had closed down at Newcastle and every toilet seemed to be backed up, lending a faint odour of disinfectant and piss to the proceedings.

Then there was Lucy. She'd studiously avoided his questions so far.

"Not here," she'd said, several times now. But Dave kept asking, kept insisting.

I knew the old bastard too well. He wouldn't go without humiliating me -- not without good reason.

Finally Lucy gave in, but not without looking around to make sure nobody was eavesdropping -- family business was to be kept quiet, kept in the family.

Like father like daughter.

"Nobody knows how it happened," she said. She leaned over the table towards Dave and lowered her voice. "There was a board meeting - Dad was submitting proposals for a wholesale modernisation of the farm."

Dave was surprised to see tears in his sister's eyes. He wanted to comfort her but a sudden laugh from the next table caused him to stiffen and hold his peace. That was more of the old man's conditioning.

Never let them know what you're feeling. It gives them an advantage.

She went quiet as a squaddie rose from the table across the carriage from them and loudly announced he was *going for a wazz*. Lucy flinched, her sensibilities offended, even more so when the squaddie dropped her a wink on the way past. She waited until the soldier was out of earshot, dabbed at her eyes with a handkerchief and watched the scenery roll by for long seconds before continuing.

"Nobody knows what happened in there. They were still there at ten o'clock when the secretary finally gave up and went home. But nobody else did. A cleaner found the bodies early yesterday morning."

That did make Dave jump, so much so that he almost spilled the cold coffee he'd been cradling since Darlington.

"Bodies? You mean it wasn't just Dad? I thought it must have been a heart attack - he was certainly due one. How can there be *bodies?*"

She tried to speak, but it caught in a hitch in her throat, and the tears were back. It took several more dabs of the handkerchief before she could continue.

"Murder, that's what it was. No, more than murder. Butchery."

"What do you mean - butchery?"

But there was to be no reply. She sat back and stared out of the window. Dave knew the signs - conversation was over for a time. He watched her for a while - the thick curve of her neck, the square jaw and the steely eyes. He had to turn away - she looked too much like him. He certainly didn't want to press her. Her rages were legendary in the family, almost as bad as the old man's.

Dave still didn't know why he was sitting there. She had phoned him yesterday afternoon.

"I've got some bad news for you." When those words were said every possible catastrophe short of nuclear war went through his mind in less than a second, so when she told him that the old man had died he was almost relieved. Almost. He was sure the old bastard would find a way to harangue him from beyond the grave.

"I want you to come with me and stand with me at the

funeral," Lucy said.

Dave had a sudden mental picture of all three of them in a car, Dad driving, his dead fingers still giving a two-finger salute to any other driver with the gall to get in his way.

"You can come, can't you? Your holidays start soon, don't they?" There was a tone in her voice Dave had not heard there before. If he didn't know her better he would have thought she was about to beg. "I've organised the transport and everything."

"I hope you got the most expensive service available," Dave said. "You know what he was like."

"Oh Dave" she sighed, sounding so disappointed, and so like his mother that he gave in. She said she'd pick him up in the morning, and Dave had proceeded to get more drunk that he'd ever been in his life. At first it was a sense of relief, a final freedom from tyranny and abuse. But after a few more beers he'd got maudlin, telling anyone in the bar who would listen about his childhood, both highs and lows. Then the self-disgust had kicked in and he'd started on the whisky. Things had got a bit hazy after that. He had a vague memory of standing in the middle of an otherwise deserted public park, screaming his rage at a father who would never again be around to hear it.

I never even got the chance to tell him to fuck off.

The hangover was starting to fade now, but the rage was still there. He thought it always would be. He stared out the window as they went through Edinburgh, Kirkcaldy and Dundee without him seeing any of them.

Finally Lucy spoke again.

"I'm glad you came," she said, and touched his hand, almost a gesture of affection. Then, as if embarrassed by any show of weakness, she went back to studying her reflection in the window. She didn't speak again until they were standing on the platform at Aberdeen station, waiting for a connection to Inverurie.

"Dad made me executor of the Estate," she said, as if it was a topic they had just been discussing. "We'll have the reading of the will after the funeral."

"I won't be staying around for that," Dave said. "I came

because you asked me to Lucy. I'm here for you, not him. If you think I'm going to sit in that draughty house while some old wrinkly goes through a list of my faults before deigning to give me a fiver then you've got another think coming."

"He *did* love you," Lucy said quietly. "He loved us both."

"Bollocks. He was a miserable old bastard who never thought of a single soul other than himself. I might just hang around for a bit after the funeral -- but that'll only be for as long as it takes me to piss on his grave."

And that was that. Dave got the stony-faced silent treatment all the way to Inverurie - giving him plenty of time to reflect on what life could be like free from the old man.

Freedom. I don't know what the word means.

Growing up had been one long round of rigidity and conformism. Don't do this, don't do that, don't get dirty, don't speak before spoken to -- just *don't*. Dave ended up living most of his life inside his head, in fantasy worlds of knights and dragons, cowboys and Indians, Britons and Saxons. And in all of them, the enemy always had the same face, the round, moon-shaped scowl of his father.

The old man had made his fortune in livestock, or rather dead stock. At the time of his death he was Chairman of the biggest venison producer in the country. He was a self-made man, rising from farm laborer to pig breeder, abattoir manager to veal exporter and on, ever upwards. Once upon a time he had wanted Dave to follow in his footsteps.

"Get out and get some blood on your hands," he said. "It'll make a man of you."

And, until Dave reached the age of eight, he honestly thought he might be able to follow the old man. Then he came home early from school one day to an empty house. For once he had some time on his own, and he used it fruitfully, kicking a football against the iron door of the garage in the backyard, taking a small joy in the fact that some of the neighbours might even be annoyed by the *crash* and *boom* every time the ball hit the target.

Of course the old man had arrived right on cue, turning the

corner into the yard just as the ball hit the centre of the door with the loudest *clang* yet. The ball rolled away and Dave didn't bother going after it. There was no point. He wasn't surprised when Father lifted the football and turned away. He only had to say one word - *Come.* Dave followed. He didn't have a choice.

That was the first, and only, day that Dave was allowed into the cold room. At the time they were running a butchering business from a shed out back. Dave knew there were *things* hanging from hooks in there, but he'd never once been tempted to look. Today Father was making sure he had to. Dave was led into the cold barn and forced to stand there while the old man took a big knife from a sheath and drove it through the football.

The ball deflated with a soft fart but Dave didn't dare laugh.

"It's time you found out what's important around here," the old man said, and handed Dave the knife. He turned Dave round and pushed him towards where a row of pigs hung from hooks.

"One slash across the throat, then another through the belly," the old man said, making swishing moves with his arms as he spoke.

Dave hadn't moved, couldn't move. He was transfixed by the sight of a dead eye staring accusingly at him and he could only stand there, the knife hanging loosely in his hand. Hot tears formed at the corners of his eyes.

"Well. Do it boy. Time to grow up."

But he couldn't, no matter how much the old man ranted and raged. In the end the knife was taken off him. There was a *flash* of silver and Dave tasted blood in his mouth, felt it *spatter* in hot spots on his face. He had thrown up even before the entrails started to coil and roll in a slow moist *plop* to the ground.

Dave couldn't stop crying, and it was the tears more than his disgust that set the old man against him - for life. For the rest of that summer the old man had berated Dave, pacing around the living room, hurling abuse at the top of his voice.

"You're no son of mine," he said, so often that most of the time Dave came to believe it, came to wonder whether maybe he was a changeling, swapped for the real son at the time of the birth.

During his Father's *little turns* Dave would squeeze his eyes shut until the tears came and the man stormed off in disgust. Dave retreated further into his inner world, forever trying, and failing, to slay the monster.

The very next term his mother got him a place at boarding school. He would have been happy but for having to go home to face more abuse every mid-term and holiday.

"You're no son of mine," had become the old man's mantra, and he chanted it every day, driving Dave further away with every word. The old man had never hit him, but Dave would carry the scars until he died.

By the time he was fifteen he'd achieved some kind of inner calm that allowed him to let the abuse wash over him. He took to staying at the school, preferring its empty corridors to the too-busy rooms at home. Mother sometimes came to visit, but his father had given up on him completely. The old man made a new will leaving everything to Lucy, and after their mother died, worn out and old before her time from having to cater to the whims of a tyrant, Dave swore he would never see the man again.

It was a vow he'd kept for five years now. The very thought of having a *father* rarely crossed his mind, so for the man to have died was no great loss. But Lucy needed him. He'd stand by her at the funeral.

But I won't shed a single tear.

~-oO0Oo-~

Detective Inspector Roberts was having his second bad day in a row, and he had a feeling he still hadn't seen the last of them. He'd got the call yesterday morning just as he was getting out of bed.

Multiple homicide. Not exactly words to bring joy to a policeman's heart.

The young WPC who had to make the call had faced the brunt of his morning grump before the import of her words had set in. That, and the mention that a Davis family member might be one of the victims, was finally enough to get his attention.

He'd known it was going to be a bad one from the looks on the faces of the younger officers. For many of them it was their first ever murder, never mind their first *bad* one. Roberts had mentally hardened himself on entering the room, putting on a protective shell that had served him well for many years during his stint in Glasgow. But even years of seeing the atrocities that drunks and addicts could afflict on each other hadn't prepared him for *this*.

He hadn't been able to stay in that room long. Just long enough to know it was a *mess* of epic proportions. After that the time had been one long blur of interviews, statements, tears and recriminations.

And we still don't have a suspect.

From where he sat now, in an adjoining office, he only had to look to his left to see two white-suited forensic men on their knees scrutinising the carpets.

Looking for bits.

Above the men the walls were splatter-sprayed with blood, and on the boardroom table there sat, neatly wrapped, cellophane packets of what looked like meat... of a kind. Five separate piles, red and wetly glistening through the wrapping with the occasional streak of pink fatty tissue showing. Roberts knew, although he couldn't see from where he sat, that it was even worse than it looked from here. While he'd been standing in the room, his back to the knocked-over projector screen, he'd caught a glimpse of *something* and moved to have a closer look at the parcelled *meat*. Two eyes had looked back at him from the middle of a pack. But that wasn't the worst thing.

One of the eyes was blue, the other dark brown,

They're from two different people.

He'd beat a strategic retreat from the room on his first visit, walking slowly, trying to keep his face impassive to set an example for the younger men. But inside he was screaming, and even now, more than a day later, he could feel the panic just waiting to take hold of him. He put his head in his hands and moaned softly.

Why me?

He'd been a copper long enough to know that murder could happen anywhere, at any time. But since leaving Glasgow more than three years ago he'd been mercifully spared most of the degradation he'd seen in the city, and he'd almost come to believe that he would be able to coast comfortably to a long anticipated retirement.

Whoever had caused the bloody carnage in the boardroom had put paid to that dream. A case like this was going to attract all kinds of attention, from the top brass, from the public, and from the press. The Scottish Highlands were in for a *cluster-fuck* of epic proportions.

And I'm right in the middle of it.

He ran his hands through his hair and wondered if he still had the will to see the job done properly. He'd got used to the slower pace of life here, the quietness and the solitude seeping into his soul. It had been a long time since he'd had to face much more than a domestic disturbance or a case of teenage vandalism. To be thrust once again into the howling face of *real* evil was going to be a strain on his already ageing faculties.

But who else is there? The others are all too young, or too soft. They've never faced anything like this before. No old man -- it's time to stand up and do what you signed up for in the first place. There's a bogeyman here to be caught.

A soft knock on the door disturbed his reverie. Looking up, he saw Sergeant MacLeod standing there. The man looked sick around the gills and had the air of someone who would rather be anywhere else but here.

I know just how he feels.

"Unless it's good news, I don't want to hear it," Roberts said. But he already knew what was coming wasn't anything good.

"Best cover your ears then Boss," D.S. MacLeod replied. "Forensics have drawn a blank so far. No prints, no fibres, no signs of forced entry..."

Roberts interrupted him.

"And no murder weapon. Christ, what a mess."

Roberts ran his hands through his hair again. Suddenly he felt overwhelmed with tiredness, as if he hadn't slept for a week.

And it might be a week yet before I see a bed again.

"Have we got ID. on all the victims yet?" he asked.

D.S. MacLeod shook his head.

"Jessie confirmed who was at the meeting. But it'll take DNA tests to ID. the... the..." The Sergeant became even paler and looked nauseous. He nodded towards the packets of meat on the desk. "...you know what I mean?"

Roberts spared him having to spell it out.

"Aye son. I know," he said softly. "How is Jessie?"

The Sergeant seemed relieved at having a different topic of conversation, although his eyes kept returning to the meat on the table as he spoke.

"She's still heavily sedated. It's a hell of a thing for a cleaner to walk in on."

"A hell of a thing for *anybody* to walk in on," Roberts said. He too couldn't look away from the meat, nor get his mind off the implications of what had been done.

MacLeod's voice dropped to a whisper.

"Have you ever seen anything like it guv?"

Roberts stood and stretched his back before replying.

"Son, I don't think anybody's ever seen anything like it. It's a mess all right. And it's all ours."

He had one last look at the packaged meat, and a cold shudder ran through him. His copper's instincts told him that this wasn't the last *meat* he'd be encountering on this case.

Time to get to work.

"Make sure there's somebody there when Jessie is ready to talk," he said. "We'll need a full statement from her."

D.S. MacLeod nodded. He seemed less agitated now that he had been given something concrete to attend to. That was something Roberts knew of old. The best thing for a squad on a case like this was to keep them all working hard, and stop them thinking -- in particular stop them thinking of the *meat* in the boardroom.

Now all I have to do is get myself to do the same.

"Anything else to report?" he asked the Sergeant.

The Sergeant shook his head.

"Not yet. Forensics will be working on it for a while. It's like a giant jigsaw puzzle... with bits missing. The only bit of luck we've had is that the press haven't got wind of it yet."

"Thank Christ for small mercies," Roberts replied. "Things are bad enough without having that bunch of vultures camped at the doorstep. That's a diversion we can well do without."

He made for the corridor, studiously averting his eyes from the boardroom.

"Any news on the next of kin of the Duncan man?"

MacLeod checked his notebook.

"They should be at the house in Inverurie around now Boss. Want to talk to them right away?"

Roberts shook his head.

"Maybe later. For now I need a smoke. Are you coming for some air?"

"I'll get myself a coffee," the Sergeant said, trying and not quite succeeding in raising a smile. "I've been standing too close to you. My mouth tastes like an ashtray."

The Inspector couldn't find it in himself to be flippant in return.

"All I can taste is blood. Too much blood."

One of the forensic team looked up as they passed the boardroom door. He shook his head. He didn't have to do anything else -- Roberts knew what it meant.

No clues, no leads - up shit creek without a paddle.

He lit up a cigarette as soon as he stepped outside the door and onto the car parking area outside the office. On the way in he'd been in too much of a rush and hadn't taken in his surroundings. It was his first time on this particular site, and as he smoked he surveyed the area.

The office sat in the courtyard of what had once been a large old farm building. It was obvious that a lot of money had gone into modernising the landscaping and paved area, and squat modern sheds spoke of more money being spent, and recently. Two police cars and a white van sat in the yard, but apart from Roberts everything was quiet and still, with nothing to tell of the massacre in the boardroom above.

He took a deep draw of the cigarette, and coughed. He tried again, but it only made the cough worse. Disgusted, he ground the butt out beneath his heel. The gravel scraped, the sound too loud in the quiet yard.

An answering clatter, like wood on metal, came from inside one of the sheds.

Roberts walked towards the shed, then stopped. Silence had fallen again.

Maybe just some wind, banging a branch against the shed.

He turned away, his hand automatically reaching for the cigarette packet in his pocket.

The noise came again, louder this time, closer. This time there was a definite rhythm to it.

That's no wind in the branches. There's somebody there.

And whoever was there, they had crossed the cordon to get in. All the staff had been sent home the day before, and the only people being allowed in were police and forensics.

If it's a fucking reporter I'll have his card.

He was more cautious now as he walked toward the source of the noise. It wasn't *just* reporters he had to worry about. He knew from experience that killers often returned to the scene of their crimes. Sometimes they were compelled to see what they had made. In some ways he hoped it *was* the killer. He was close to bursting with the need to make someone pay for the atrocity in the boardroom, and his hands curled into fists at the thought of dishing out some rough justice.

"This is a crime scene. You shouldn't be in there," he shouted. He had now identified the source of the noise at least. It was coming from the large shed directly in front of him.

The clattering rose to an almost frenzied drumming, echoing around him as he reached the shed. Roberts pushed open the huge sliding door, having to put his shoulder into it while it squealed and complained.

Everything fell silent as he walked into the shed. It was an abattoir, all gleaming metal hooks, stainless steel troughs and flenshing blades. Everything looked sparkling and clean, as if it had just been washed out with hot water and soap, but the smell was there - it would always be there - the faint tang of old blood and fear. He took a step inside, bracing himself for the possibility of an attack.

Nothing moved.

"Hello?" he shouted, feeling self-conscious in the large open area. Suddenly it felt like he'd farted in church. Indeed this empty space with its echoes of blood and death did remind him of fire and brimstone sermons in cold churches in his childhood.

In the far corner a black shadow shifted. Roberts started to move that way. The shadow seemed to run the length of the far wall, something grotesque and misshapen. The clattering returned, louder than ever. Roberts felt like he was trapped inside an oil drum while a maniac hit the outside of it with a hammer. His patience was growing thinner by the second.

"Come on out of there son. I don't have time to be playing hunt the dickhead."

Everything went quiet again. Roberts walked further into the abattoir.

The shadow ran across the far wall. All of Robert's pent up frustration came out in a shout.

"You're cruising for a bruising son. When I catch you, you'll get a size twelve boot up your arse."

He was answered by another sharp rattle of wood on metal, like a drum roll.

Everything fell still and quiet, again. The place went cold, a sudden temperature drop that sent a thin frost across all the metal surfaces, and once more Roberts was reminded of the cold stone of a church floor on winter mornings. He stood still, seeing his breath in the air in front of his nose.

A footstep sounded -- right behind him. He turned, raising his hands, aware even as he did so that he was too late to stop an attack.

D.S. MacLeod put a cup of steaming coffee in his hand.

"What are you doing in here Boss?"

Roberts looked around the shed. The frost had gone as quickly as it had come, and everything was once again quiet and still.

~-oOOOo-~

They'd got to Inverurie in the early afternoon. The journey from Aberdeen had been a silent one. Lucy was still giving Dave the full cold-shoulder treatment but that was something he was *long* used to - it had lasted nearly three weeks in the past, so he was more than prepared to wait. They got a cab from the station but the trip took less than two minutes before it deposited them in the driveway of a two-story house.

Dave had been expecting something less grand than the imposing building into which Lucy led him. The house looked like it had stood on the spot for centuries, its grey stone merging almost seamlessly with the soil underneath and, although the wind was biting and chill, a real log fire blazed in the hall he was led through. It was only as she was entering the main room that Lucy finally spoke, and her tone was terse and cold.

"The farm is about five miles away - out in the sticks." Her nose actually lifted in the air, as she forgot that their house in Derbyshire, *Dad's folly*, was at least six miles from the nearest large town. Dave didn't get time to enlighten her. "The police station is out that way as well. We'll go there tomorrow morning if they don't contact us first," she said.

Dave was shown to a bedroom where he unpacked his bag - it didn't take long. He changed into a clean pair of jeans and a heavy pullover to inure himself against the chill of the Highland air and headed downstairs to find a drink. He was to be disappointed. The large drinks cabinet in the main room was locked tight, and there was no sign of Lucy. He opened and closed doors to cupboards, pantries and lavatories until he found a large country-style kitchen. Father obviously had someone *doing* for him, as the place was neat and tidy, with all the cupboards well stocked with tins, dried rice and beans, cake and biscuits. The fridge was also well provisioned, with meat, eggs and milk.

But still no booze.

He went back upstairs and rapped on Lucy's bedroom door.

"Go away," she shouted. "I need some peace and quiet. I'll make us something to eat later."

It wasn't eating that Dave had in mind. Now that the hangover was gone he found that more booze was *exactly* what he required to get through what was turning into a trip down all his yesterdays. It occurred to him that the booze was the one thing he shared with the old man, a thirst that was hard to quench.

I'll thank him in hell.

He made another sweep of the downstairs rooms, and tried the drinks cabinet again, in case it was just stiff. But to no avail. He fetched his jacket and went out in search of oblivion. The sound of the door slamming behind him was like a gunshot, and he faintly heard Lucy shout, *Bastard!* That improved his mood as he walked out into the road and looked around.

At four o'clock on a Saturday afternoon the place was deserted. It looked to be a tidy enough little town, but it was far too quiet to be anywhere where Dave could stay these days. He'd spent enough time in his own head as a boy. These days he preferred noise and crowds, places where he could lose himself among others -- places where he didn't have too much time to think - places not like *this*. The place was empty, with only the occasional old lady wrapped tight in an overcoat suggesting it wasn't a Sunday. He wandered for a while, but didn't find a bar and the thought of a pint of cold beer had grown big in his mind. He made his way back to the taxi rank at the station and collared the nearest driver.

"I'm looking for a pub that's open," he said.

The driver looked him up and down.

"Are ye sure ye're old enough to be drinking?" he said, but there was a smile on his lips as he said it. "Get in. I know the feeling when you've got a thirst."

"Just the one," Dave said. "Just a quiet pint is what I'm after."

The driver laughed.

"I wish I had a pound for every time I've heard *that* line. Do ye know where ye want to go?" he asked as he started the car.

A name came to mind, a town Dave had only ever read about in Lucy's letters. He remembered something about *lunch in a local bar.*

"Monymusk?" he said. "Is there a pub there?"

The driver laughed again. "So, the toon's fame has even spread to England has it. Aye, I'll take ye to Monymusk - but don't be expecting anything fancy."

The man drove like a demon, the needle approaching eighty on long straight stretches of road, only going below fifty on the corners. Dave watched the scenery and tried to seem nonchalant. He didn't know what he'd been expecting - rugged hills, heather and cliffs were known from the television, but this corner of Scotland was green and lush, only occasional glimpses of distant mountains reminding him he wasn't in Derbyshire. The cabbie kept up a constant flow of chat, but at such a speed and in such an accent that Dave caught less than half of it. He contented himself with grunting replies, hoping that he wasn't agreeing to anything he shouldn't.

They flashed past a thirty-miles-per-hour speed limit sign doing sixty, and Dave had a vague impression of a row of houses on either side of the road when they suddenly screeched to a halt outside a tiny whitewashed cottage.

Dave paid the driver, and got a business card in return.

"Give me a bell when ye need to get back," the driver said. "It doesn't do ye much good to be walking these roads in the dark."

With that he left, the car bulleting off into the distance.

A cold wind whistled around Dave's ankles, blowing a solitary crisp packet along in its wake. This town was even quieter than Inverurie. There was not a single person on the streets and there was no sign of life - not even a wisp of smoke from a chimney. But the small white cottage had a battered sign outside -

The Twa Dugs, and the windows displayed faded posters for beers that had long since disappeared from the market.

It's the beer I'm after, not the ambience. Any port in a storm.

He headed inside. The place was so quiet that Dave thought it might be closed - the television was switched off, as were the fruit machines, and there was only a solitary light above the bar. He had already turned to leave when a voice called out.

"Can I help ye sir?" The barman poked his head above the counter. "I was just stacking some bottles. Taking advantage of the lull in custom as it were."

He threw back his head and laughed, his humor so infectious that Dave had to join him.

"Pint please," Dave said.

"Lager, Light or Heavy?"

That had Dave stumped. A short lesson on ordering beer in Scottish pubs later and him and the barman were getting on famously. The first beer went down quickly.

"Another please?" Dave said.

"Coming right up." The barman paused while pouring the beer, as if unsure whether or not to say anything, then seemed to come to a decision. "I was sorry to hear about your father," he said.

Dave felt as if his afternoon had just lurched into the Twilight Zone.

"You know who I am? I've never been here before."

The barman shook his head.

"Aye. You have. The old man used to bring you up here when you were a wee lad on your summer holidays."

Dave took a long gulp of beer.

"I don't remember that... I mean, I remember being in Scotland on holiday... But I don't remember him ever taking me anywhere - let alone him taking me to a bar."

The barman gave Dave a fresh beer and took his money. He went to the till to make change, turning back to speak.

"You were just a wee fellow at the time. But the old man was so proud of you. He showed you off every chance he could. You were in here often. I kent you as soon as I saw you."

Dave was non-plussed. None of this fitted with his view of how his world had worked back them.

"You knew the old man well then?" he said.

The barman nodded.

"Aye. We all knew him around here. He came in two or three times a week. He liked his malt whisky, that he did. It was a shock to hear the news."

Dave took this as a sign that the man would say more.

"Is there anything you can tell me about what happened? My sister says the police are keeping things tight to their chest."

He knew immediately that he'd pushed too hard. The barman suddenly looked like he'd rather be anywhere else.

"Sorry son. I only know what's going out on the jungle drums. Something about bodies being found up at the slaughterhouse. That's all I've heard."

His eyes told a different story. Dave tried again to push him.

"Come on. A small place like this? There must be *some* gossip going around."

The barman turned away, heading off down the bar.

"We're not all sweetie-wives out in the sticks. We keep ourselves to ourselves. Your father knew it. That's why he liked the place."

Dave was suddenly angry.

He's actually defending the old bastard.

"He got to play lord of the fucking manor. *That's* why he liked this place."

Again the barman shook his head.

"He was a good man. Many around here will tell you that."

Dave laughed bitterly.

"He was a ruthless bastard."

The barman was still having none of it.

"The man's not even laid in his grave yet. Show some respect."

The barman made a point of walking to the other end of the bar and started cleaning some glasses that looked to have been cleaned already.

Dave dove into the beer, taking large swallows.

Looks like that conversation is over.

Over the next hour the bar slowly filled up and Dave's beer kept coming.

He tapped an empty glass on the bar.

"Another please," he said, not hearing the slur in his own voice.

"I think you've had enough son."

"Nonsense. I'll have another beer," Dave said. He raised his voice and looked around the bar. "Or would you rather talk about what happened at the abbatoir?"

The whole bar went quiet. The barman had a pained look on his face. But Dave got another beer.

A wizened old man who had been in the corner seat for a while rose and took the stool beside Dave. He looked like he'd been wallowing in a mud bath for several days and when he smiled he had more gaps than he had teeth. He offered a hand to shake.

Dave took it gingerly.

"Name's Jim. Jim Rogers. Do ye mind if I join ye? We don't often get strangers hereabouts...and I like to talk to somebody different. Round here they've got nothing on their minds but farms and farmers. It makes for boring conversation."

Dave shuffled his stool over to make more room. Jim motioned the barman over and made a swirling motion with his hands above their glasses.

"Same again here when you've got time," he said, and turned back to Dave. "Ignore the smell son. It's the animals. I work over at the slaughterhouse. I'm the *mucker oot* of the pens where they keep the deer. Blood and guts everywhere, runnels of it, mixed in wi' shit and....hey, watch out."

Dave suddenly felt like he was about to throw up and he swayed on his stool. He nearly fell until Jim put out a hand to steady him.

"Don't mind me," Dave said sheepishly. "I've got a thing about blood."

He grabbed his beer and sent half of it down to tell his

stomach who was Boss here. The little man at his side did the same with his own. Dave's earlier conversation with the barman came back to him.

Maybe the old man knows something.

"I've heard something was going on at the place. Wasn't there a story on the news?" he said, trying to sound casual.

The old man lit up, eager to talk.

"Oh aye, it was on the television right enough. A one woman show if you catch my drift?"

Either the drink had got to Dave, or the old man was talking in riddles.

"What do you mean?"

Jim tapped the side of his nose knowingly.

"The auld Mither looks after her own."

The barman cleared his throat noisily and the old man stopped talking.

He took another long, almost guilty, slug from his beer and waited until the barman was at the other end of the bar before resuming. He leaned forward and spoke softly, almost a whisper.

"They say she got them all in less than a minute. Tore out their lights like a knife through butter. They say..."

The whole bar suddenly fell silent.

Jim looked up to see the barman standing directly in front of him.

"Right Jimmy. I think you've had enough."

"I was just telling the lad a story..." Jim started, but the barman didn't let him finish.

"The lad doesn't need your stories. He's not just a lad. He's mourning his faither."

Jim went pale.

"He's that boy?"

The barman nodded. The old man dropped his head, got carefully off his stool and left quietly without saying another word.

"What did he mean?" Dave said, having to struggle to form a sentence. "Who is this woman he was talking about -- this old mother?"

The barman took the beer glasses from in front of Dave and washed the contents down the sink before replying.

"The ramblings of an alcoholic. You shouldn't listen to old Jimmy. Last week it was wee gray aliens in his bedroom. As for you wee man," the barman said to Dave, "I think you'd best be getting on home - you've got your old man's funeral to arrange."

It was only when Dave was out in the fresh air that he realised he didn't know where he was. The cold air had combined with the alcohol and it drove all coherent thought away. His feet started taking him along the road. He had no plan, no thought other than to walk. He'd get somewhere - eventually.

Everything became jumbled in his mind - the squaddie winking on the train, the drinking , both here and back at Uni, the railway platform at Aberdeen, all became a swirling mosaic of images. And in each one a face leered at him, a round, moon-like face, his old man, jeering at him even from beyond the grave.

The next thing he knew it was some time later. He was standing by the roadside, heaving up the contents of his stomach. He felt strangely better after that. He did his best to clean up his face, hoping he had kept his clothes slime-free, and finally stood up straight and looked around. He stood at a crossroads, and along all four branches there was only darkness and the soft brushing of the wind in the trees.

Sobriety caught up with him. Somewhere along the walk and the subsequent proceedings he'd used up most of the effects of the booze. He was also completely lost. No, it was more than that - if he had been in a city he could have found his way to some recognisable landmark, but here he could see nothing. He looked upwards, searching for the stars, but that was a vain hope - he couldn't even tell which was the North Star and which was a planet. A full moon leered down, taunting him.

He was about to head down one of the roads - any road - when there was a sound behind him, just at the limits of his hearing, a rough rasping as of stone against stone. He turned.

An old woman stood, no more than three yards away. Dave's

first thought was that he was back in his booze-induced reverie again, for he was strongly reminded of his old Grandma, who had died when he was six. All he remembered of her was the thick black mourning garments, and a smell of lavender. The woman in front of him was equally old and bent with age, equally clad in thick black velvet draped over a small frame.

But there all resemblance stopped. And the smell in the air, even overpowering the taste of vomit in his throat, was one of animal mustiness.

As yet the old woman had paid no attention at all to Dave. She bent over and lifted something from the verge of the roadside. He could see there were deep pockets sewn into her clothes, the contents of which clattered as she moved, as if full of stones.

She bent again to pick up something and study it with such intensity that she was as still as a marble statute then, with a movement so quick he almost didn't catch it, she transferred whatever it was from her hand to her mouth. She stood upright as Dave watched, the fine silver wings of her hair wafting in the breeze from under a headscarf so enveloping as to be almost a hood. He was about to call out to her when she turned, and his shout, already turning to a scream, was caught, frozen in his throat.

There's no face.

That was his first impression. There was just a black void so deep he felt he was falling into it. Then her hand came up and pushed the hood away from her head, and this time Dave did scream, a scream echoed by the thing in front of him.

Her face wasn't a face. It was a construction, a mask of bone and hide stitched together with thick twine that glowed white in the dim light. Beneath the mask something moved - a squirming as of a tribe of maggots in dead flesh. He would have run then, but the eyes held him, deep blue eyes sunk deep beneath the mask eyeing him with cold appraisal.

"So," a voice said, even though the lips of the mask were sewn tight. "Are ye your father's son, or are ye your own man? Are ye a herdsman or a butcher? It's make your mind up time." And she cackled, like a crone in a Disney cartoon. She stretched a hand out to Dave. It seemed to have been stripped of flesh until all that was showing was bone.

Dave backed away - a reaction that brought more cackling.

A cloud went over the moon, throwing them into sudden darkness. Dave's eyes took seconds to adjust, and when they did he was once more unsure of the extent of his sobriety. The old woman still stood in front of him, but the black velvet of her clothes had taken on a blue, luminescent tinge such that she *glowed*, a ghostly wavering aura all around her that seemed to waft in the wind like the wisps of hair. She stretched out a hand again, the blue glow even more prominent where it ran along the white of the bone.

"Are ye your father's son, or are ye your own man?"

The bone *clacked*, and Dave remembered old Jimmy's words from back in the bar

Tore out their lights like a knife through butter.

He tried to back away but came up hard against a cold stone wall. She followed, the piercing eyes never leaving his.

"Please," Dave said, dismayed at the whine he heard there. "I don't know what you want."

She cackled again.

"Are ye a herdsman or a butcher?"

A thin film of frost *crackled* as it ran all along the wall behind him and stretched across the road for yards around.

Suddenly the crone's face was lit by car headlights. She blinked, and Dave blinked, and when he looked back she was off and away. Her skirts rose up, exposing ankles ending in a pair of thick, cloven hooves. She turned ten yards down the road and pointed her hand at Dave. He saw the five long, serrated bones reflecting the faint moonlight as the cloud moved on. The glinting edges looked perfect for slicing meat.

"It's make your mind up time," she said, in a whisper that he heard even above the sound of the approaching car. He looked to the car, then back along the road.

The old woman had gone.

The cab driver rolled down his window and shouted out.

"Alan at the bar phoned me, and telt me ye were out on the road. Get in and I'll take ye home."

It took long seconds to sink in, and even longer for Dave to recognise the cab driver.

"Come on son. I haven't got all night."

He got in and the driver took off, going if anything even faster than before. Dave didn't speak, he couldn't, his mind was still full of the sight of those fingers and hooves and the words the crone had spoken.

Are ye your father's son, or are ye your own man?

He thought he'd known the answer to that, but the events of the day were starting to make him doubt himself. The old man had marked him in so many ways, and he was finding new scars all the time.

The driver didn't speak until they reached the house in Inverurie.

"I would stay in for the rest of the night," he said. "It's a night for the Mither. Ye don't want to meet her twice."

He screeched away, leaving Dave on the gravel path.

Still dazed, Dave stood for a long time looking at the night sky and wondering, until the chill brought him to his senses and sent him scuttling for warmth. Suddenly he felt stone cold sober and in more need of a drink than ever. Checking his watch he was surprised to find it was still only late evening - there would still be a bar open somewhere. But the thought of walking strange roads had lost its appeal. Besides, there was a light on in the main room, visible as a warm glow of yellow through thick curtains. That meant someone was in, and that the drinks cabinet might be finally accessible. He turned his back on the night and headed inside. There was a comforting murmur of conversation coming from inside the main room as he pushed open the door.

And stopped all talk dead in its tracks.

There were only three people in the room, and they had all just gone quiet. The silence lasted just two seconds before the woman with her back to Dave turned.

He hadn't recognised his sister until that point. Her perfect facade had been severely dented - her hair hung in limp strands, tangled as if clawed with a trembling hand. Her make-up was a faded memory, streaked and running around her eyes. The effect was to age her by years, making her look like the vulnerable child Dave dimly remembered. As she rose from the chair she looked so much like their mother that Dave felt a hitch rise in his chest.

"What's wrong?" he asked, touching her shoulder. He was amazed when she collapsed sobbing onto his chest. He held her awkwardly, unsure where to put his hands - they'd never been in this position before now. Her sobbing turned to full scale crying. Dave looked over her shoulder. The other two people in the room were young uniformed police officers, and both were pointedly looking at the floor. Finally Lucy raised her face towards him, fresh tears running down her cheeks.

"They won't let me bring him home," she sobbed. "They won't even let me see him."

He looked at the nearest policeman, who looked up and gave an embarrassed nod.

Dave petted Lucy's hair as if he was stroking a dog. "It's okay," he said softly. "We'll probably have to wait until after the post-mortem." He looked at the policeman for confirmation, but the officer was looking even more uncomfortable now.

"What's the problem?" Dave asked.

The officer sighed and, before replying, looked at his partner for confirmation to proceed.

"As I told your sister, we cannot release the bodies until.." he paused, as if struggling for words. "Until we've decided which parts belong to which victim."

Lucy began to howl, a high-pitched keening like a bird in pain. Dave gently sat her in an armchair and turned back to the policemen.

"Tell me," Dave said, then, when they showed signs of prevarication, "Please, just tell me. I'll have to find out sometime."

The younger of the two looked pale and ill, but it was he who spoke first.

"Have you ever seen a butcher strip a carcass, so efficient that everything is packaged into parts?" He gulped, suddenly having difficulty swallowing. "Well, that's how it was. Four men and one woman to start with, around four hundred kilos of meat after. I don't think you need to know more."

Dave sat down hard, feeling dizzy. The images in his mind were back, but this time it was of a dead pig, spinning on a hook as entrails *flopped*, steaming to the ground.

The policeman was still speaking, but Dave had missed something.

"...keep this information confidential until we find the killer?" The officer looked at Dave, and Dave nodded, hoping he'd made the right response. Then the meaning of the officer's words sank in.

"You mean you haven't caught him yet?"

"That's why we need your help - you, and your sister's. We need access to company records, and I believe you two are the new owners. I'd like you to come down to the factory with us. There may be something there that will point us in the direction of the killer."

"Now?" Dave asked, and received a double nod in reply.

"No," Lucy moaned, "I can't. Not into that place. Not where..." She broke down again, her sobbing so quiet as to be almost inaudible.

Dave knelt by her side. "Come on. You need to rest," he said, and helped her up out of the chair. She clung to him as if he was a lifebelt in a stormy sea.

"Give me a minute," Dave said to the policemen, and led Lucy out of the room and up the stairs. She was a dead weight in his arms and he was almost carrying her as they reached her door. He leaned her against the jamb and pushed the door open.

"I'll deal with the police," he said, herding her into the room. She rubbed at her eyes, hard, as if disgusted with herself, and nodded, but something was gone from her eyes, something that had made her Lucy.

She might never be the same again.

She fished in her handbag. He thought she was looking for a fresh handkerchief, but she produced a bundle of keys that she handed to Dave as if she never wanted contact with them again.

"These are for the office - the filing cabinets and desks and such. They'll find what they want in this lot."

Dave had already turned away when a soft word drew him back.

"Dave," she said, and she was definitely not the same woman Dave had left earlier. "Please be careful. I can't lose you as well."

There were tears in her eyes again as Dave hugged her close.

"Don't worry big sis," he said softly. "I'm not going anywhere."

The policemen were waiting in the hall when he got downstairs.

"Can't this wait till morning?" he said. "It's all been a bit of a shock."

They used a line he thought only applied in the movies, and he had to fight back a laugh -- once he started he might not be able to stop.

"This is a murder investigation, sir."

He followed them out of the house and round the side of the house to where a patrol car sat in the shadows under the trees. A minute later they were barrelling along dark country roads.

Sitting in the back of the car Dave felt like a criminal, and the silence from the men in front only reinforced his isolation. He wanted nothing less than to find a bottle and dive into it -- but Lucy's tear stained face kept coming to mind. He'd made her a promise now, and despite all that had happened over the years, she was all the family he had.

I can't let her down. Not her.

He leaned forward in his seat, peering between the officers -- it made him feel less like a prisoner.

"So have you any clues?" he asked, trying to keep the anxiety out of his voice.

"No," the younger policeman said. "It'll probably be some

of them loonie lefties." Now they were away from the house his accent had began to re-assert itself. "We're hoping that there'll be something in your old man's files - threatening letters or some such nonsense."

Nothing more was said until they drove through Monymusk - Dave saw the white wall and the still-lit facade of the pub as they passed and felt a pang of thirst - and pulled up in the drive of a converted farm building. The policemen led Dave along a corridor to a room with yellow crime scene tape stuck in an X across the open doorway. The walls and windows were covered in a frenzied splatter, a Jackson Pollock frieze of blood. Sitting on the table was a pile of cellophane wrapped packages, full of red, glistening, meat, like a butcher's sale at a fair.

Dave couldn't take his eyes off it. He felt the old nausea rise in him and he had to turn away and hold onto the doorjamb for fear of falling over.

Are ye your father's son, or are ye your own man?

The younger policeman pulled the boardroom door shut.

"Sorry sir. You weren't meant to see that. Come into the main office. The cabinets we need you to go through are in here."

"I still don't see where how this will help," Dave said.

The young policeman lowered his voice.

"Sometimes these killers like to send messages beforehand -- threatening letters and stuff."

"The old man wouldn't have had any truck with any of that," Dave said. "He'd have burned the paper to ash and pissed on it."

"Please sir, just try," the policeman said. "We need any lead we can get on this."

The lad - younger even that Dave himself - looked as much in need as Lucy had.

Seems like it's my night to be a good Samaritan.

Dave nodded and made his way into the office.

He almost turned and left again - the whole place *reeked* of the old man, from the pictures of his businesses over the years to the golf trophies, from conspicuous displays of his charitable endowments to photographs of him with prominent people. There was no way to escape the tyrant - not in here.

But the young policeman was just outside the door, and Dave wasn't about to show just how *weak* he really felt. He turned back and started going through the files, slowly at first then quicker as he realised that most of it was just office admin -- and boring office admin at that.

He went through every desk drawer and filing cabinet in the office over the next half-hour before opening the last desk drawer. He found a bottle of malt whisky, and a thick manila envelope. He took to the whisky first. There was a glass - crystal of course - in the drawer beside the bottle and he poured himself a stiff measure, downing half of it in one gulp and letting the fire warm his belly.

He sat for a while turning the envelope over and over in his hands before finally opening it. It proved to be a thick printed proposal for the upgrading and mechanisation of the farm. He turned pages that showed fleshing machines, massive, pristine, blades gleaming on the page, huge industrial mincers and plans for the slaughter and packaging of huge numbers of animals.

He heard the Hag's words again.

Are ye a herdsman or a butcher? It's make your mind up time.

He was about to put the proposal down when several sheets of paper fell out from near the back. He made to stuff them back in, then realised they were notes written in his father's painstakingly neat script. He read while sipping the rest of the whisky.

~-oOOOo-~

T he first sheet was just a short note.

"She was here again last night," it began, and Dave almost gave up there and then, but another sip of the whisky allowed him to continue. "I have no idea what she wants, or what she is, but she is most insistent. I must be on my guard."

And that was all it said. The other sheets were more densely packed, and looked to be a series of notes - research even - on the mythology of old hags in Scottish folklore. As Dave read his sips at the whisky became more frequent. One passage in particular caught his eye.

She is also known as Beira, Queen of Winter and is renowned for the making of many mountains, built as she strode across the land dropping pebbles from her pockets, all the while herding the deer, fighting the coming of Spring, and freezing the ground.

Dave thrust the papers back into the proposal. He'd read enough, and now he was thinking too much, about pockets in black velvet aprons, and a thin layer of frost on the tarmac.

The younger policeman came back in just as Dave was considering making a new dive into the whisky bottle.

"Did you find anything that can help us sir?"

Dave stood, too fast, and the room threatened to spin. He held onto a filing cabinet for balance.

"No.... And I think I've had enough of this place. Where's your superior officer. I need to find out when we can bury the old man."

"Sorry sir," the officer said. "There's another call just come in that the D.I. needs to deal with."

~-ooOOoo-~

D.I. Roberts *really* didn't want to get out of the car. .
"It's torn up bad," they'd said.
He could already see it in his mind's eye. *Torn up* was something he'd seen more then enough of in Glasgow, a city where the knife, or *chib*, was the weapon of choice of every daft boy with a chip on his shoulder and rage in his heart. There were nights when all he saw in his dreams was blood and tissue - on the outside of bodies they should be inside. He didn't need to see any more, didn't want to see any more.

As the car drew to a halt in a remote lane on the outskirts of town, Roberts considered leaving Sergeant MacLeod to deal with it. But that would be admitting to himself that the fear had got the better of him, and in all his years as a copper, that had *never* happened.

Not until tonight.

He pushed the thought away and got out of the car. MacLeod was waiting for him, and led him over to where a young constable stood over a body.

"What have we got son?" Roberts said to the constable.

"We got the call from somebody who said he thought a dog had been worrying sheep." The lad looked down, and went pale. "Instead I found this." He threw a hand over his mouth and lurched off to one side, starting to retch.

MacLeod bent down to study the body while Roberts lit a cigarette to cover the smell of blood and vomit. It didn't help.

"Anybody we know?" he asked as MacLeod studied a face that was little more than scraps of flesh hanging off exposed muscle and jawbone.

"I think it's wee Jim," MacLeod replied. He lifted a bloody scrap of material away. "He's got a jacket like this one, and the body looks to be the right size. But it's hard to tell. He's cut up bad."

"Like the others?"

"Not as cleanly, but I'd say so, yes." MacLeod paused and bent closer. "There's something here."

He reached forward to the body, intent on picking something out of the carnage, but Roberts stopped him.

"Best not to disturb anything else. Leave it for forensics."

He bent down beside the younger cop and peered closer. A single length of bone seemed to be *stuck* in the victim's chest, wedged between ribs exposed to the air and near where the heart had been forcibly torn from the chest cavity.

It looked remarkably like a finger.

Christ. I need a drink.

Ten minutes later Roberts and MacLeod stood at the bar. It was just past closing time, but nobody was being allowed to leave.

"So, Wee Jimmy was in, but he left early? That's not like him, is it?" Roberts said.

The barman started washing glasses, and didn't look the police in the eye.

"Leave that alone while we're talking to you," Roberts said, almost shouting. "Did the wee man argue with anybody?"

The barman was still fiddling with a dishtowel.

"Not that I noticed," he said.

"Did he talk to anybody in particular?"

"Not that I noticed."

"Did he seem agitated at all?"

The barman started to say something, but Roberts interrupted him.

"No... wait... Let me guess..."

He turned to the rest of the people in the bar.

"How about you? Are you any more observant?"

All he got in return was blank stares.

MacLeod spoke up.

"What's wrong with you lot tonight? I thought the wee man was your pal?"

Still no one answered.

Roberts led MacLeod out, and left one parting shot.

"Just as well we're not on fire son. This bunch wouldn't even pish on us."

Matters didn't improve any when they got back to the squad room.

The press had finally got wind there was a story to be had, one with gore, local politics, skullduggery and mayhem. The corps of press were gathered around the station, salivating at the thought of juicy titbits to come.

They can stay hungry. There's no way I'm going to feed the frenzy.

He was pinning pictures of the latest victim on the evidence board when D.S. MacLeod came in carrying a heavy plastic evidence bag with the bone *finger* inside.

"The forensics have been over this Boss," MacLeod said. "But you're not going to like it."

"Just what I needed," Roberts replied, almost falling into the seat behind his desk. "More good news. Well don't keep me in suspenders son... Let's have it."

MacLeod sat down opposite the D.I. He put the plastic bag on the table between them and pointed at it.

"It's bone... mammalian bone. And it has been sharpened at one end. It's razor sharp."

"This is the murder weapon?"

MacLeod nodded.

"Looks like it Boss. But it's got the forensic guys stumped."

"How's that?"

"Look closer."

They bent over for a close-up look at the bone. At one end, there was a mass of torn blood and sinew, still looking fresh and damp.

"It looks like this was forcibly torn from a hand during the attack on wee Jim."

Roberts tried, unsuccessfully, not to think of the brute strength required to do the amount of damage they'd seen using this bit of bone as the weapon.

"We're looking for somebody with a mangled hand?" he said, hoping against hope that there was an answer he could *believe.*

MacLeod took a few seconds to reply, as if he wasn't sure of what he was saying.

"Not somebody guv. *Something.* The bone's not human. Not even close."

Roberts ran his hands through his hair and sighed deeply.

"It's a wind up. It has to be."

Once more MacLeod shook his head.

"Forensics don't think so. They say it's kosher. A real mystery."

Roberts banged his fist on the table, hard enough to hurt.

"Well I'll tell you what it's not - it's not the fucking Twilight Zone. I won't have any *mumbo-jumbo* clouding the issue here. We've got a killer to catch, before he does it again."

He stared into space for long seconds before continuing searching for an inner calm that seemed an awfully long way away.

"What about the Duncan boy? Anything there?"

"The lads said he was a wee bit drunk, that's all. And clean. Whoever did the wee man would have been covered in blood."

"Bugger," Roberts said. He went to light a cigarette then remembered the station was a no-smoking area. "I had him down as prime suspect for the boardroom mess. Everybody knows he hated his old man."

"Aye. But he was hundreds of miles away. He couldn't have done it."

Roberts chewed on the unlit cigarette.

"There's something going on that we're not getting," he said. "Did you check on the other employees?"

"Yes Boss. All accounted for."

"Well thank Christ for small mercies. Go home, get some sleep. We'll start talking to them in the morning."

They left the squad room and turned off the light. Neither of them noticed that the bone in the plastic bag glowed in the dark, faintly fluorescent blue.

~-oOOOo-~

Dave woke feeling groggy and unsure of where he was. It took him several seconds and two failed attempts to stand to remember.

When he'd got back from the farm he'd found Lucy in a drunken sleep on the sofa in the main room, the dregs of a vodka bottle on the table in front of her. It took most of his strength to get her upright and up to her bed. She hadn't woken, had only moaned softly. He let her flop, fully clothed on the bed then pulled a quilt over her.

"Daddie?" she whispered, and that was enough for Dave. He left at a hurry, closing the door softly behind him. By the time that was done, he'd wanted more booze.

Lots more booze.

Luckily Lucy had opened the drinks cabinet. He'd made serious inroads into a bottle of whisky before tiredness finally overwhelmed him. He too had gone to sleep on the sofa Now, sometime in the early hours of the morning, he was seriously unsteady as he forced himself upright and opened the big bay windows, taking gulps of cool fresh air.

The events of the previous night seemed little more than a blur of alcohol fuelled nightmares; the wee man in the pub, the back of the police car, and the old crone on the dark road. He'd lost all sense of perspective, and was starting to worry about his own sanity.

Grief does things to people.

He'd heard it said often -- it was just that he never expected to feel anything other than relief at the old man's passing. He stepped out into the garden and looked up at a clear, starry, sky above. But even there the full moon's face leered down at him, reminding him of old abuses. He moved to go back inside.

Rasp!

The sound came from behind him, a rough scraping as of stone against stone. He turned towards it. The Hag stood no more than three yards away from him. The contents of her pockets clattered as she moved closer, and she spoke in a soft, lisping highland lilt.

"So… Are ye your father's son, or are ye your own man? Are ye a herdsman or a butcher? It's make your mind up time."

She seemed to *roll* backwards from him, one smooth movement as if she was slowly pulled away, lost in the darkness of the garden before he could blink. Dave staggered back into the room and finished the whisky in two gulps before collapsing, comatose once more, on the sofa.

~-oOOOo-~

T he morning found D.I Roberts and D.S. MacLeod sitting on a sofa, awkwardly holding tiny china cups of tea. Jessie, the abattoir cleaner, was sitting opposite them in an armchair, staring at the fire. The woman looked on the verge of fresh tears. It was obvious from the puffiness around her eyes that she'd done plenty of crying already.

The policemen looked out of place in the small immaculate living room, stocked full of dainty floral prints, china ornaments and ranks of photographs of children and grandchildren. They sat perched on the edge of the sofa. Roberts didn't know about MacLeod, but it felt like it wouldn't be safe to sit back -- the thing looked like it was ready to swallow the unwary.

They'd been here ten minutes now, and still hadn't got anything useful from the woman. Every time she started to tell her story she burst into tears and wracking sobs so loud that the china plates hanging on the walls rattled in sympathy. Finally, just as Robert's patience was reaching breaking point, she started to speak, the words coming fast as if she was hurrying before fresh sobs overtook her.

"I wasn't even supposed to be there," she said quietly. "Mary Campbell changed shifts with me."

Sergeant MacLeod perked up and raised his head from where he'd been studying the tea for the past five minutes.

"Did she do that often?"

Jessie shook her head.

"That was the first time in years. She'd got some stupid thought about the place being haunted... something about an old woman in a black dress. But Mary's never been the full shilling, even when we were lassies... I remember when..."

Roberts nipped her in the bud. It didn't do to allow Scotswomen of a certain age to get too far off topic. It might be hours before you got back.

"Jessie," he said softly. "The office?"

She acted as if he'd just slapped her.

"I told you already. And you saw for yourself... them packages, all laid out like meat. And the eyes..."

She stopped, started to cry again, then wiped the tears away. MacLeod gave her a few seconds before prompting her.

"We just wondered if you'd remembered anything else? Anything that might help us catch the killer."

She continued to dab gently at her eyes with a handkerchief

that had seen better days.

"I haven't slept right since. Everytime I close my eyes I see that meat... and hear that noise."

Roberts started to pay closer attention. His *spidey-sense* had started to tingle, the old copper's intuition that he'd just heard something important, even if he wasn't yet sure why it had any bearing on the case.

"Noise?" he asked. "What kind of noise?"

Jessie stared into the fire, remembering.

"Drumming. Like wood on metal. When I was walking along the corridor towards.... towards..." She paused again, thinking. Fresh tears squeezed out and ran down her cheeks. "Anyway, that's when I heard it. What a noise. Like somebody banging with sticks on a metal barrel."

Roberts joined her in staring into the fire, remembering the sounds in the abattoir.

Sticks?

Or bone?

~-o0O0o-~

D ave was still asleep on the sofa when Lucy entered and walked across the room. She kicked an empty whisky bottle as she passed, and the sound it made as it clanked up against the stone fireplace started to rouse him from his stupor. She opened the curtains, letting morning sunlight wash into the room before grabbing him by the shoulder and shaking him fully awake.

"You didn't sleep here all night?" she asked as Dave opened one eye warily and moaned as sunlight lanced like a spike into his brain. "Did you?"

He came awake slowly, rubbing at his temples and groaning. He looked down at the whisky bottle.

Finished it! A job worth doing is worth doing well.

"I suppose I must have done. Just don't let me do it again. Bad dreams."

Lucy moved around the room, tidying up the evidence of the night's drinking. If she was suffering any after-effects of her own binge she wasn't showing it. She had her shell back on, bolstered by the activity.

"Best get yourself tidied up. John Fraser is coming round in half an hour."

"Who?" Dave said. His brain was refusing to get in gear, and he was starting to wonder whether more whisky might help things along. Lucy didn't give him enough time to head for the drinks cabinet.

"Dad's solicitor. Given the circumstances he thought we should have the reading of the will early."

"I told you. I'm not interested."

Lucy's voice took on a pleading tone.

"Please? I'm hanging on by a thread here."

The shell dropped so quickly it was like seeing her break in front of his eyes. She had tears in her eyes, and looked so lost, so bereft, that Dave couldn't refuse her.

"Give me half an hour. Put the coffee on would you. The blacker the better."

He made his way slowly to the bathroom and stood in front of a mirror checking out his bloodshot eyes.

Well that was a great idea.

As usual after a night on the booze, he was ready to swear off it for life. But he knew better than that. Even after only two years at University it was apparent that he had a thirst that took a good deal of quenching, and he knew that it wouldn't be long before he had the first of the day - *just to get me going.*

But first he had to get rid of the remnants of the day before. He undressed and got into the shower, pulling the curtain across. The room steamed up fast, the heat seeming to draw alcohol from his pores. At the same time he felt the memories, both real and imagined, flow away. By the time he'd finished scrubbing he felt almost human. He got out of the shower, grabbed a towel and turned.

"Make your mind up," was written in jagged writing across the condensation on the mirror, the letters already starting to run in small streams down the misted surface.

You've got to be fucking kidding me.

Dave wiped the message way quickly. That way he might be able to pass it off as another booze-induced hallucination. But it wasn't going to be that easy. The mirror cleared to show the old crone standing behind him, a bony hand reaching for his shoulder. She *cackled* in his ear.

He turned, almost too fast, sliding on the damp floor. But haste wasn't needed.

There was no one in the room but him.

~-o0O0o-~

D.I Roberts and D.S. MacLeod faced each other over two mugs of coffee. They'd come to the local cafe, more to get away from the job for a few minutes than anything else. Roberts played with his cigarette packet, and the girl behind the counter kept eyeing him warily, ready to admonish him if he even *tried* to light up. D.S. MacLeod had barely spoken a word all morning, and he obviously had something on his mind. Roberts was prepared to sit and drink as much coffee as it took to find out what it was.

MacLeod finally broke his silence.

"You've been here what... Three years now guv?"

Today, it feels longer. Much longer.

"Nearly four," he replied.

MacLeod nodded.

"More than long enough to notice that they're a superstitious bunch around these parts?"

The Sergeant looked serious, but Robert tried for levity. He had a feeling he knew where this was going, and he didn't want to hear it.

"Too many long dark nights and not enough women," he said. "And..."

"And too many sheep," MacLeod said, but he still didn't smile. "Aye, we've all heard the jokes. But it's the stories I'm talking about -- the old stories, the ones that make the hair stand up on the back of your neck. And in these parts, there's none older, none scarier, than the tales of the auld Mither."

With that the Sergeant lapsed back into silence. Roberts ordered two more coffees and got another glare from the waitress as she moved his cigarettes aside to put the mugs down. MacLeod waited until the girl was out of earshot before continuing.

"If you talk to the intellectuals, they'll tell you she's a Jungian archetype, the old wise crone who knows all your secret desires. Others will tell you that she's a remnant myth, an old Goddess fallen on hard times since the coming of Christianity. But that's just for the theorists. Round here, they know her as all too real."

Roberts made to protest, but the Sergeant put up a hand.

"Hear me out Boss. I need to get this off my chest. The farmers in these parts have always known her as a protector of the countryside -- Mother Nature if you like. She turns up in old stories and songs all over this part of the country."

"So how come I've never heard of her?" Roberts asked.

"Because if you talk about her, you die a horrible death," MacLeod said softly. "At least, that's the story."

The implications of that started to sink in. There might not be an *actual* Auld Mither... but there might be someone pretending to be her.

"And you think somebody's using the story as a cover to commit the murders?"

"Aye, maybe guv," the Sergeant said. He lowered his voice to a whisper. "But what if there's some truth in the old stories? What if she's *real*."

"What? Ghosts and ghoulies? Halloween fancies for the terminally naïve -- that's all they are."

"Aye... But what if...?"

Roberts' patience snapped.

"You mean, what if I'm next on the list for talking about

her?" He waved his hands theatrically. "Oh, I'm so scared. Oops, watch out - I think I've shit myself."

He left the Sergeant to the coffee and went in search of a place where he'd be allowed to smoke without chastisement.

~-oOOOo-~

D ave almost ran into the front room. All the time he was getting dressed he'd kept his eye on the mirrors, but there was no return of the *hallucination* - if that indeed was what she was. He was starting to get back more memories of the night before, and his encounter outside the French windows.

Are ye your father's son, or are ye your own man? Are ye a herdsman or a butcher? It's make your mind up time.

He was intending making straight for the drinks cabinet again - so intent that he almost didn't notice that the room was already occupied. Lucy was sitting in one armchair, and a sharp-suited elderly gentleman was in the one opposite her. Lucy looked up as he entered, and he saw the concern flash across her face.

"Are you okay Dave?"

He pushed down his rising panic. Lucy looked even worse than he felt, and she'd had more than enough grief to deal with already.

"Yep. Why shouldn't I be?" he said, trying for nonchalance but hearing the whine again.

"I'm sorry to intrude on your grief," the suited man said. As he spoke Dave realised that this must be the solicitor Lucy had mentioned earlier.

He certainly looks uptight enough.

"No, go right ahead," Dave said. "We're up to our armpits in intruders today anyway."

That got Lucy worried again, and he immediately wished he hadn't spoken. He headed for the drinks cabinet and poured himself a large whisky, ignoring the steaming mug of coffee that had obviously been left for him on the table between the chairs.

"Don't mind me. I'm just a bit frazzled," he said as he

downed the whisky in one.

The solicitor lifted a small briefcase into his lap and took out a piece of folded paper

That must be Dad's will. Here comes the humiliation.

"This won't take long," the solicitor said. "It's just about the shortest will I've ever seen."

"I can guess," Dave said bitterly. "Lucy gets everything, right?"

The man smiled, but it never reached his eyes.

"Your sister gets the house," he said, then paused for effect. "He left you the abattoir. His offshore accounts are to be split equally between you, but after death duty and other taxes there'll only be around thirty grand each for you from that."

It took a few seconds to sink in, and even then Dave couldn't believe it.

"The abattoir? What the hell would I do with that?"

"He thought you'd say that," the solicitor replied. "He said that in the event of you refusing, it will revert to Lucy. All you'll have is the offshore account cash."

Dave poured himself another whisky.

"She's welcome to it. I'll take the cash though... it'll help pay for my education - which is more than the old bastard was willing to do when he was alive."

Lucy looked shocked.

"You can't turn it down. It's disrespectful."

Dave knocked the whisky back and reached for the bottle again.

"You know what they say? Like father, like son."

~-o0O0o-~

D.I. Roberts reached the end of his tether at lunchtime that day.

"Enough of this pussying about," he said to MacLeod. "Let's get out to the abattoir and rattle a few cages. If they think they're scared of the *old mother*, just wait till they see me in a snit."

He lit up a cigarette in the car on the way, and MacLeod, after taking one look over, wisely kept his mouth shut. They pulled into the car park at the same time as a local taxi. A slightly dishevelled woman got out.

"Miss Duncan?" MacLeod asked. "You *are* Miss Duncan?"

Lucy Duncan nodded.

"I'm D.S. MacLeod," the Sergeant said. "And the D.I. here would like to talk to your staff."

Roberts kept quiet. He didn't trust himself to keep his temper for too much longer.

"Come on in," Lucy said. "I've called a staff meeting so everyone will be there. I'm sure they'll be only too happy to help."

"I wouldn't bet on it," Roberts muttered as he followed her inside.

I hate being right all the time.

It was half an hour later and Roberts' face was grim as the staff shuffled sullenly out of the room leaving Lucy and the cops alone.

"I'm sorry," Lucy said. "I don't know what's got into them."

The meeting had been a complete washout. All Roberts' questions had been met by a stony, almost fearful, silence.

"Fear and superstition," MacLeod said. "It's a potent blend."

"Well I'm sorry anyway," Lucy said. "You've made a trip for nothing."

Roberts could feel his temper rise to boiling point and struggled to push it down.

I've had just about as much of this shit as I can take.

"I'm not done just yet," he said. "They might open up if we get them one on one."

He turned to face MacLeod.

"You take the office workers… I'll head out to the sheds. Wee Jimmy's drinking buddies have got some explaining to do."

~-oO0Oo-~

Dave was making serious inroads into the contents of the drinks cabinet when the French windows burst open from the outside. The black shape of the Hag bounded in along with the glass. She leapt on him before he could breathe, knocking him to the ground, sitting on his chest and staring down at him, the blue eyes unblinking behind the mask of sewn skin. Razor sharp bone clacked in front of his face and Dave flinched, expecting at any second to be carved open.

"It's make your mind up time."

The ivory-white hand reached for his face.

Not like this. Please. Not like this.

She suddenly stopped and sniffed at him, like a dog after some food. She sat back, lifting the hand away.

"You're not the one. Not anymore."

And as quickly as she had come, she was gone, back out into the garden beyond the French windows.

Dave lay there, trying to catch a breath, his head pounding with the sound of blood, as if a mad drummer had taken up residence. It was several seconds before he could bring himself to move. He turned his head. The will lay nearby on the floor, fluttering slightly in the breeze coming in the open windows. The import of the Hag's words finally hit him.

You're not the one. Not anymore.

He left the room at a run, shouting his sister's name.

~-oOOOo-~

Roberts was getting nowhere. So far he'd spoken to three men that had been in the pub last night, and none of them were talking. The fourth was to prove no different. Roberts knew Alex Price well -- they lived only three houses apart on the same street, and spoke often in the newsagents where they both indulged their nicotine habits. But today the man was acting as if Roberts was the enemy.

Name, rank and fucking number. Time to take off the gloves.

"What's all this nonsense about noticing nothing in the pub

last night Alex? You were with the wife, weren't you?"

The man nodded sullenly. Roberts pushed harder.

"I thought so. And we both know that nothing gets past her... She knows every single thing that's gone on for the past forty years. So tell me... what really happened? Why is nobody talking? Come on man -- your pals are getting slaughtered. Have you no conscience?"

Alex Reid looked around to make sure no one else was listening. His voice dropped to a whisper, and he leaned forward so that there was no chance of being overheard.

"That was the problem Mr. Roberts. Wee Jim was talking too much. Everybody in the bar heard him."

"Talking about the Mither you mean?"

Reid looked rapidly from side to side, eyes wide in terror.

"I shouldn't have said anything."

"Away with your havering man," Roberts said. "I've been talking about the bitch all morning, and I'm fine."

Reid made to leave but Roberts grabbed him by the shoulders.

"You're going to tell me what's going on here, or by Christ I'll knock it out of you. Then I'll kick the auld bitch around town for afters."

Reid squealed like a trapped animal.

"You shouldn't mock her Mr Roberts. She's just looking after her own."

Roberts allowed all the rage and frustration to rise up in him.

"Her own? You mean the folk around here? The folk who'll let a wee man get brutally murdered and not lift a hand to help catch the killer?" He leaned forward, shouting in the man's face. "If you're her own, then she can go fuck herself, she's no mother of mine."

Reid pulled himself out of the D.I's grasp.

"You've said too much Mr Roberts," he said in a hoarse whisper. "You've said *far* too much."

Above them there was a rattle, a drum roll of bone on metal.

"I told you," Reid shouted. "I fucking told you."

He fled, wailing.

Roberts looked up to where the noise had come from.

"Come on then. It's time we stopped all this voodoo bullshit. Come and fight a real man."

A shadow moved quickly across the ceiling.

"Enough already. I'm here," Roberts shouted.

A soft singsong voice spoke at his ear.

"So am I."

Slash.

Roberts grunted as a handful of razors were embedded in his belly.

He tried to speak, but only bubbles of blood came out.

Slash!

Roberts opened from groin to sternum.

~-ooOOoo-~

Dave burst into the boardroom to find Lucy sitting at the table. He'd spent the last half-hour hoping against hope he wouldn't be too late, and had almost frightened a poor cab driver to death with his screamed demands to go ever faster. By the time he arrived at the boardroom he was flushed and out of breath.

She looked up from a pile of papers on the table.

"Oh.....I suppose you've changed your mind?" she said. "Well you're too late. I've told the staff I'm taking over. They took it rather well I thought I..." She stopped, stunned as Dave grabbed her and started to drag her out of the room. "Stop it. You're hurting me."

I've got no time to explain.

He responded by dragging her faster. She squealed in pain as he felt something *wrench* in her shoulder.

"Sorry," he finally managed to say, but didn't stop dragging her out into the corridor. "But we have to get out of here. We..."

At the far end of the corridor a black shape scuttled into

view, little more than a shadow. The sound of clacking bones echoed along the narrow passage.

Shit! Out of time.

He turned to Lucy. She was looking at him as if he had gone insane.

Maybe I have.

"I want the factory," he said before he had a chance to change his mind. The sound of clacking bones turned to drumming, the walls shaking as the Mither beat her rhythm against them.

"Quick. We're out of time. Can I have it?"

Lucy looked puzzled.

"Of course you can...didn't I say so?"

"Say it again."

"The factory's yours if you want it."

Dave shouted along the corridor.

"Do you hear that? It's mine. I want it."

He turned and ran, leaving a bemused Lucy staring after him.

Dave looked back. The black shadow of the Hag scuttled along the corridor, coming fast. White-boned fingers scraped gouges into the walls, the *scraping* cutting through Dave, a high screech that rose and rose until it howled like a storm in his head. He could do nothing but flee, down long empty corridors with the Hag chasing. He looked back again, just once.

She's catching me.

The thought gave him added impetus. He burst through an exterior door and sprinted outside. The sun was just starting to go down, and black shadows loomed all around. Behind Dave there was a clack of bone, still getting louder. He turned and ran again -- straight at the large double door of a shed.

Suddenly everything went quiet.

The door was slightly open and the sound it made when he pushed the sliding doors open echoed loudly in the night. He slipped inside, trying to keep quiet, but the noise of the door opening had woken the shed's occupants. There was a shuffling and a sudden lowing.

Several hundred pairs of dead eyes turned and stared at him. The deer were packed in rows, so tight that flank and rear touched, rears stained and packed hard in brown, vile muck.

Clack!

Bones clattered behind him.

Dave turned. The Hag was right there behind him in the doorway.

"Are ye your father's son?" she said. "Or are ye your own man? Are ye a butcher?" Razor sharp fingers waved in front of him once more, clacking together like diabolical scissors. "Or are ye a herdsman? Make your mind up."

Dave looked at the bones, and then back up at those unblinking blue eyes.

"My father didn't deserve what you did to him!"

The Hag didn't reply. With a wave of her arms she indicated the animals in the pens. "Are ye a herdsman or a butcher?"

She waved the bony hand in front of his face again, and bones clattered.

Like father like son? Bugger that for a lark.

"I'm my own man," he said, realising, almost for the first time, that he actually believed it. He moved through the shed, opening all the locks. Many of the animals seemed unable to move, but with a bit of coaxing he got them out of the shed and herded them into the field beyond.

Clack!

The bones clattered behind him. He turned to face the Hag.

"Now you're a herdsman," she said. "Your own man."

She lowered her head and bowed to him, twice, before heading off across the field. The herd followed her, heading over the brow of the hill, their forms outlined in black against the deep red sky beyond.

The Auld Mither looks after her own.

Printed in Great Britain
by Amazon

21459250R00031